THE STORY OF YOU

hardworking

creative

Sincere

curious

generous

Kindness

honesty

THE STORY OF YOU

loving

courageous

thoughtful

By
Lisa Ann Scott

Illustrated by
Sue Cornelison

BOYDS MILLS PRESS
AN IMPRINT OF BOYDS MILLS & KANE
New York

You're writing a story
with everything you do.
What's this story about?
It's the story of you!

When you choose to be kind,
when you decide to share,

when you reach out a hand,
when you make sure it's fair,

you're writing the
story of you.

When you are bold and brave,
　when you choose something new,
　　when you try though it's hard,
　　when you learn what to do,
　　　you're writing the story of you.

When you ask for a hug,

when you offer one too,

when you're first to step up,
when you find a new view,

you're writing the
story of you.

When you search and explore,
when you hatch a big plan . . .

. . . when you find
your own beat,

when you shout,
"Yes, I can!"

you're writing the
story of you!

When you offer to help,
when you make awesome things,

when you meet a new friend,
when you try out your wings,

you're writing the story of you.

When you're not sure what's right,
when you're filled with regret . . .

. . . when you can't find your voice,

when you're mad,
don't forget,

you're writing
the story of you.

When you say what is true,
when you're jealous, but cheer,
when you're scared, but speak up,
when you're lost, but still steer,

you're writing the
story of you!

When you show what you know,

when you follow your heart,

when you do your own thing,

when you're ready to start,

you're writing the
story of you!

When you share the best you,
when you break from the crowd,
when you make a hard choice,
when you feel strong and proud,

you're writing the story of you!

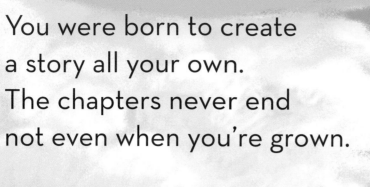

You were born to create
a story all your own.
The chapters never end
not even when you're grown.

The story of you tells
the world who you are!

So what happens next?
That's up to you.
You *are* what you do.

You're the star in this story of you!

To my two sweet kiddos, it's been a joy
watching you write your own stories.
   —LAS

For Nika, Ezra, Alder, Evren, Harper, Hayes,
Holden, Lincoln, Sam, Kinsley, Kaden,
Jax and Luka with love.
Choose to be courageous, curious,
and creative, but above all else,
choose kindness and love,
for the choices you make, make you.
I am excited to see your stories unfold.
   —SC

For information about permission to reproduce selections from
this book, please contact permissions@bmkbooks.com.

Boyds Mills Press
An imprint of Boyds Mills & Kane, a division of Astra Publishing House
boydsmillspress.com
Printed in China

ISBN: 978-1-63592-311-7 (hc)
ISBN: 978-1-63592-470-1 (eBook)
Library of Congress Control Number: 2020949130
First edition
10 9 8 7 6 5 4 3 2 1

Design by Barbara Grzeslo
The text is set in Frutiger.
The illustrations are done digitally with ink washes.